JUSTIN MEETS ZIP AND ZAP

Written by

Martha M. Harris

To
Wright

Martha M Harris

AuthorHouse™
1663 Liberty Drive, Suite 200
Bloomington, IN 47403
www.authorhouse.com
Phone: 1-800-839-8640

AuthorHouse™ UK Ltd.
500 Avebury Boulevard
Central Milton Keynes, MK9 2BE
www.authorhouse.co.uk
Phone: 08001974150

First published by AuthorHouse 6/29/2006

ISBN: 1-4259-3298-3 (sc)

Illustrations by Stephen Adams

Library of Congress Control Number: 2006904808

Printed in the United States of America
Bloomington, Indiana

This book is printed on acid-free paper.

Bloomington, IN Milton Keynes, UK

authorHOUSE

Dedicated
To
My Grandson

Tyler Keesey

Look up in the sky! What's that I see?
A very strange object: What could it be?
It can't be an airplane; the shape is all wrong.
It doesn't have wings, and it's round and not long.
Its engines are roaring, this monster from space;
And it shines bright, colored lights all over the place.
It's coming much closer. Can it really be
That this strange-looking object is landing by me?
Now I see it much better. It's a spaceship, I'm sure.
Should I be afraid? Should I look any more?
It's too late to run; there is no place to hide.
I might as well stay and see what's inside.
Now that it has landed, I see a strange face
Of someone who surely must live out in space.
He passed by the window. He opens the hatch.
Now I see two little strangers—that match!
They are coming toward me. I'll tell them my name.
Then maybe they'll just do the same.

"My name is Justin. I live on this land.
I want to be friendly. Will you shake my hand?"

"Yes," he said, while tipping his cap.
"It's a pleasure to meet you. He's Zip and I'm Zap.
We just came to visit. We live out in space.
Some elves said that Earth is a very strange place.
But you can't always believe what you hear from the elves,
So we thought we would come and look for ourselves.
It is lucky we found you; we need a good guide.
Would you like the job? If you would, hop inside."

"It's a really great offer, but surely you know
I must ask my mother if she'll allow me to go."

"Mom, can you hear me? I have a surprise!
I know you will hardly believe your own eyes!
I have two little friends who are different from most.
Why, Mom, you look like you just saw a ghost!
You don't need to be frightened. I promise you that.
They have come here from space. One's Zip and one's Zap."

"We came here from space to tour your great land,
And if Justin could guide us, it would simply be grand.
Our spaceship is sturdy, and we fly it with care.
We think it's a chance he can't get everywhere.
Well, what do you say? We hope it's good news.
We think it's an offer you just can't refuse!"

"It sounds like a very good chance, I can see,
For a young boy to travel around, and it's free.
But I think the idea would have much more appeal
If I went for a ride and then see how I feel.
There is something else that I need you to know.
We must take Justin's sister along when we go.
I will just be a moment; I must go inside
And tell Jenny that we will be taking a ride."

"Oh, Jenny, come quickly. I have a surprise!
We are hopping a spaceship to sail through the skies.
Don't be afraid; don't cover your face.
These are just two little strangers from space.
Justin, perhaps if you take hold of her hand,
She'll relax with your friends from a faraway land."

"Come on, Jenny, there's no need to fear.
My friends Zip and Zap are visiting here."

"If everyone's ready, we'll all climb inside
And see how you like your first spaceship ride."

"Now fasten your seatbelts. I'm sure they all work.
Sometimes the spaceship takes off with a jerk.
The engines have started; the pathway is clear.
Just look out the window while Zip and I steer.
We're climbing up higher, up into the clouds.
We're leaving the noise, pollution, and crowds."

"Well, how does it feel, Mom, to be here inside,
Having this perfectly wonderful ride?"

"I have to admit it is pleasant enough.
I had thought it might be a little bit rough.
Are you planning to just fly around here in space?
Or will you be making a landing someplace?"

"Do you think we can fly way up to the stars?
Or up to Jupiter, Venus, or Mars?
Or maybe to Mercury, or Saturn, let's say.
Or Neptune, or Pluto, or the Milky Way.
Or even Uranus is all right with me.
Any one of those places would be great fun to see.
Where did you come from? You never did say.
That's where I'd like to go for the day."

"Our planet's called Zark; it's smaller than those,
And therefore, not as well known, I suppose."

"I don't have the time to go out into space.
We really must visit a much closer place.
I think that I have an agreeable plan.
We could go visit Kim, Amy, and Deeann."

"Who are these people you want us to see?
Do you think they will want to meet Zip and me?"

"They are my cousins. They don't live too far.
It takes only six hours to get there by car."

"Visiting your cousins would be nice, it's true,
But when it's time to land, what will we do?
They don't have runways for spaceships, you know.
We will find this a problem wherever we go.
I think you'll admit it would be quite a feat
Trying to land our ship on a street.
We'll first try to find a local airport,
And if none are close by, use a field of some sort."

"There is an airport near where they are,
But to land on a field sounds better by far.
They have a large field right close at hand.
There aren't many houses near where you'd land,
And large trees around there would hinder folks' views,
For a spaceship landing is not everyday news.
And if large crowds of people come by, I would say
I would surely be quite late for work today.
For I would imagine, the minute we park,
Folks will crowd in to see strangers from Zark."

"My dear, see that object shaped like a cone?
That happens to be a Zark telephone.
So call your folks up and let them all know
We will visit an hour and then we must go."

"Let me make the call, Mom. I'd sure like to try
To make a telephone call from the sky."

"Just put the large end of the cone to your ear,
Then raise the antenna and see what you hear.
The computer is ready when you hear the Zark tone,
Then punch in the number like you do on your phone."

"Golly, it's ringing! It's easy as pie
Making a telephone call from the sky.
Hi, Kim. Look out the window if you want a surprise.
See that strange object coming down from the sky?
That's me in a spaceship with two friends from Zark.
We are planning to use last year's garden to park.
We can't stay too long because Mom is inside.
She's checking to see if the ship's safe to ride.
I have to hang up now; our landing gear's down.
In just a few minutes we'll be on the ground."

"Wow! What a smooth landing! Now my *seatbelt* is loose.
Hey, look out the window. There is Kim's new pet goose.
Open the hatch, Zip. I can't wait to *see*
The look on Kim's face when she *sees* it is me
And knows it was true when I said we would park
On last year's garden, with two friends from Zark."

"Hi, Kim. Isn't this perfectly, wonderfully grand?
Did you get out in time to *see* the ship land?
Are Deeann and Amy here with you all?
If not, you had *better* go inside and call.

"I called them. They said they'd *be* here in a flash.
I hope they don't peddle *so* fast that they crash.
They couldn't *believe* it was really true,
But they will when they *see* the spaceship and you."

"Here they come now. Look at Deeann's face.
Now she knows that we have two friends from space."

"Hi Deeann. Hi Amy. We came here from space.
We are hoping to travel all over the place.
If Justin's allowed, he will show us the way,
And we'll visit new places, day after day."

"I think it is neat! Can we go for a ride?
We've never seen a spaceship's inside.
It really would be exciting to say
We went for a ride on a spaceship today."

"You are welcome to look around the inside,
But I'm sorry; there won't be time for the ride.
Perhaps we'll come back and visit again.
You'll surely be welcome to take a ride then."

"Well, Mom, while the spaceship is here on the ground,
And Zip is showing my cousins around,
Will you make the decision and please let me know
If you feel it is safe, so I can go?"

"I've had enough time; my decision is made.
Since going for a ride, I'm no longer afraid.
I've made up my mind; I am letting you go.
So I guess you can let everyone know."

"Oh, Mother, I really don't know what to say.
This really has been an unusual day.
I can hardly *believe* the way that I feel.
I would never have thought this all could *be* real."

"Here comes Kim and Amy, and Deeann and Zip.
I guess we have come to the end of this trip.
Did you hear what Mom said? She's agreed to the plan.
She says I can travel around our great land.
It sounds so exciting. It will *be* hard to wait.
Now Mom says we must go or she will *be* late.
This certainly has *been* an *eventful* trip.
Goodbye, everyone. We are boarding the ship."

Remember, if sometime as you play with your toys,
You listen and think that you hear a strange noise,
It might be that spaceship getting ready to park,
That's been flown here by two little strangers from Zark.
And if you're allowed, you might head for the sky,
The very next time the Zark spaceship flies by.

About the Author!

Martha Harris enjoys writing stories and skits. She discovered the joy of writing as a young child and has been writing on and off ever since. She especially likes to write in rhyme. She enjoys traveling, creating crafts, and spending time with her many grandchildren. She is retired and lives in Florida with her husband Curt.

LaVergne, TN USA
18 February 2011
217042LV00002B